VARIABLE STAR

Essential Poets Series 89

Guernica Editions acknowledge the financial support of the
Government of Canada through the Book Publishing Industry
Development Program (BPIDP).

This publication was assisted by the Ministry of Foreign Affairs
(Government of Italy) through the Istituto Italiano di Cultura.

VITTORIO SERENI

VARIABLE STAR

Edited and translated by Luigi Bonaffini

With an Afterword by Laura Baffoni Licata

GUERNICA
Toronto·Buffalo·Lancaster (U.K.)
1999

Original title: *Stella Variabile*.
First published in December 1981 by Garzanti Editore.
Copyright © 1999, by The Vittorio Sereni Estate.
Translation © 1999, by Luigi Bonaffini
and Guernica Editions Inc.
Afterword © 1999, by Laura Baffoni Licata.

Antonio D'Alfonso, Editor.
Guernica Editions Inc.
P.O. Box 117, Station P, Toronto (ON), Canada M5S 2S6
2250 Military Rd., Tonawanda, N.Y. 14150-6000 U.S.A.
Gazelle, Falcon House, Queen Square, Lancaster LA11RNU.K.

Legal Deposit – Fourth Quarter
National Library of Canada
Library of Congress Card Number: 98-72808
Canadian Cataloguing in Publication Data
Sereni, Vittorio
Variable star
(Essential poets series ; 89)
Translation of: Stella variabile.
Poems. ISBN 1-55071-087-7
1. Sereni, Vittorio–Translations into English.
I Bonaffini, Luigi. II. Title. III Series.
PQ4879.E74S7213 1998 851'.912 C98-900685-9

Contents

ONE

Those Thoughts of Yours of Calamity 7
In an Empty House 8
Toronto on a Saturday Night 9
Workplace 10
Work in Progress 11
Farewell Fair Lugano 14
Women 16
Interior 17
Growth 18

TWO

Cutting and Sewing 19
Poets on Brera Street: Two Ages 20
In Venice with Biasion 21
Poet in Black 23
Revival 24
It Must Be the Boredom 26
Sunday After the War 27
Festival 29
Exterior Seen Again in a Dream 30
Giovanna and the Beatles 32
Every Time I Almost 33

THREE

A Vacation Place 34
Niccolò 47
Fixity 49

FOUR

I Was Translating Char 50

FIVE

Verano and Solstice 56
Requiem 57
First Fear 58
Second Fear 59
Another Workplace 60
The Sickness of the Elm Tree 61
On the Climb 63
The Knoll 64
Po Summer 65
In Parma with A.B. 66
The Cisa Highway 69
Rimbaud 71
Luino-Luvino 72
Progress 73
Another Birthday 74

Notes 75
Afterword by Laura Baffoni Licata 77

ONE

Those Thoughts of Yours of Calamity

and catastrophe
in the house where you have
come to stay, already
inhabited by the idea
of your having come here
to die
– and these people with their friendly smile
this time for sure
you're dying they know it and that's why
they're smiling at you.

In an Empty House

If they ever came to life. They seem to come to life

from room to room, they never really
come to life in this rainy air. What came
to life – I suddenly able to see in the air's slow brightening –
was a throng of daisies and buttercups out there.
Just so *one had*.

Just so one had a history somehow
– and meanwhile Munich in the early morning papers
ah thank goodness: there had been an agreement –
just so one had an exquisite history among the swastikas
one September under the rain.

Today *one is* – and one is badly anyway,
you yourself part of the evil
whether or not the sun and meadow get shrouded again.

Toronto on a Saturday Night

To Niccolò

and even if the trumpet just heard
– but with what power with what blond sweat –
in Toronto that Saturday night

were in the sign of Tipperary once again
it mixed abnegation and innocence

and if Toronto were but a larger Varese

with mercenary
                       or non-mercenary dedication
tearing itself apart in that gift of itself
it sought a beyond
not seeming less than the great Satchmo
ready to play to empty spaces
with a gold trumpet no less once he had landed on the moon

just so it remains an abnegation capable of innocence
        past reward

and what else does Tipperary mean
if not all the possible beyonds of dedication
 to the nothing that suddenly can
set any evening on fire
in Varese in Toronto in...

Workplace

Those steps where the stairs bend sharply, all
those people who have gone by (over and over
every day to work) turning from the stairs from life.
          Worn threadbare
by those reiterators, in that spot the carpet
lies in a cold reflection of light. Both winter and summer,
and frozen
in the ambush of a thought forever like itself
always expected for that spot
always identical,
is the gaze that invariably falls there
every day every hour
of years of work of light years
of cold – an autumn
begins there as always.

Work in Progress

I

It must be that there are lives like dead leaves –
the house amidst the waters
                                            obviously in ruins
that leprosy repressed by steel
those cobwebs of domestic sounds from only yesterday
(the beds lying empty, the couches damp, the chairs unused)
oh leave it in the flash of its enigma
expunged by traffic as it surfaces at each turn of Riverside
        Drive

don't wonder what could have ever happened to them
don't say life is carbonization or divorce
(how strange one should remember only this of an entire
        metropolis)

or trifles of a winter trip into immensity –
the jet's flutter in its mutant's paroxysm
when it still is and no longer is
a light-number flashing on New York's timetable

or even those signs painted in the lobbies of the anthills –
leafing epidemics on walls tiles wallpapers
what are those small swastikas doing here in the Bronx,
there were, there are, so many of them, they say, between
        doves and hawks
but you can also take them to be emblems old
        Indian motifs,
no matter how they branch in this half-sleep:

hangings and standards trampled in Europe
or the Indian's hopeless shadow among the skyscrapers?
others are on their way in the agony or the ecstasy
new shadows that I glimpse at without seeing
now disquiet me.

II

For some people I know it's not enough
to want me dead. They hope I die,
but in infamy. They don't know
that I have done worse that I have
miniaturized them in my memory.

But those from here are leaves
trifles signs working on a large scale
not the ones frozen in miniature those non-specialists
minimal mouths clamoring under glass
– and they would be right if they only knew –
stiffened forever in the melt
fossils in living concrete.

III

Inopportune futile untimely
the above-mentioned sprite.

Another one springs up and annihilates him
beating different wings from down there,
from the sea, if you can call a sea
that grayness of inexistence around Ellis Island
once a quarantine islet
fading into a cloud of memory:
of young Charlie
Chaplin and of those
on the waiting list with him
who knocked on the doors of the States
with all of America before them
soon overwhelmed by its first stories
of very swift shadows
of immigrants dishwashers tramps
– and today they'd make themselves over
recompose themselves
with the puffs of smoke from underground
stubbornly looking for gold as always
against the spent glasspanes
on the frost on the desert here in Wall Street
on a Sunday.

New York, 1967

Farewell Fair Lugano

quando nella notte ce ne andammo
Bartolo Cattafi

I will have to change geographies and topographies.
She will not hear of it,
she denies me in effigy, she rejects
the mirror of myself (of ourselves) I hold out to her.
But I can't help it if the road
winds under me
like a woman (like her?)
with rightful immodesty.
                              And after all
I have wells in me deep enough
to throw even this in them.
See, it's snowing now...
But I, Madam, do not appeal to the whiteness of the snow
to its conclusive woodland
                              peace
or to the warmth of ermines, braziers,
wood and waxes it subtends, with shining virtues
that are torn to absurdity
elsewhere
but wizened here, if you briefly look at them,
like sagging flags.
I am for this – nocturnal, fanciful – March snow,
        multivalent
with petals and buds in a flood among uncertain
mountains transitory lakes (like me,
howling in ecstasy at the hills in bloom?

fake-blooming, an hour of sun
will melt the frost),
for its whirlwind its tumult
that unforms night and then reforms it
laminating it with pewter, steel, light silver.
They are proud of it, the nightwalking gentlemen
who have come down to the street with me
        out of a painting
seen once, lost sight of,
pursued among the reminiscences of others
or merely dreamed.

Women

Without their knowing
the dream decided to reunite on the same evening
two or three of them
who had once been his
(after the thing had been consummated, he remembered,
he imagined getting rid of them
by elbowing, kicking them away.)
                                    The silence
fermented in the darkness of the room –
and the enticing orchard will be
but anatomy privileged by the whip of the executioner
running under the rain
inside a lager.

Interior

Enough fighting enough. We went at it
the whole afternoon out in the open.
Let's call it a tie.
The hills are being draped by the wind. Others are
already battling out there, the word
belongs to the shoots rushing at the windowpanes
to the heather to the sage
in waves more and more thick and dusky,
everything soon adrift.
Is this meant to be peace?
To get close to burning firewood
to the dying taste of bread to the
transparency of wine
where the day just down from the cliffs
somberly rekindles
with the cry of the plateaus
in the fleece of the ravines in the velvet
of false distances till we fall asleep?

Growth

She has grown in silence like grass
like the light before noon
the daughter who does not cry.

TWO

Cutting and Sewing

The toy,
sheep or lamb you patch up
by order of the little girl,
with a head stronger than its ovine
genus would suggest
is in the family with you. Your stubborn
profile in sewing up the toy
and that strong head: patient
in impatience – and your frown
which still won't let go of my life
in its pursuit of butterflies
and cliffs... For every
scratch a darn, for every tear
a patch.
   How much
is the work of a darner
worth, how much
your life?

March, 1961

Poets on Brera Street: Two Ages

It takes a century or close to it
– Ungaretti would blaze up in the doorway
of the Apollinaire gallery –
it takes all the toil all the evil
all the rotten blood
all the limpid blood
of a century to make one...

(Meanwhile
on the opposite sidewalk
two by two arm in arm
two by two hating one another in warbles
of reciprocal love
six of them were parading. Six.)

In Venice with Biasion

O God, what great kindness
have we done in time past...
O God of the night
what great sorrow
cometh unto us...

Ezra Pound

What past talent of ours
soon forgotten
earned us the gift of Venice
of its wonders?
For what great sorrow
still awaiting us
did Venice repay us in advance
by being as it was?

Such questions no longer answer
the god of the waters the god of the night.
They sink with the cities
below our horizon.

With the pain of a question not asked
of an answer not received we go
on waters perpetually troubled:
on distancing black waters, one night, conjuring
a Venice of our own amid those scattered lights.

But with his seashells
with his sea pebble comes
the boyforever the allterrestrial Biasion.
To support capitals, to space seagulls.
He doesn't like, they say, to expend himself
vertically, but is this
really true? The spike
of his solar bread soars
over shapeless outlines
over setting domes and peaks.

Poet in Black

Black belt black boots
black the floppy hat
all decked in black he sits
straight on a stool he hoists
a sign with the words: *Ich bin*
stoltz ein Dichter zu sein
barely moving his lips.
I am proud to be a poet.
But why so much black?
I ask him with my eyes.
I am dressed in mourning for you
from behind black glasses
with his eyes he answers me.

Revival

The Option is good – the small
Jew gone back to tend to his classics
greets me hastily in the wind.

Reeeally good...
Echoing it back
the gallery of crows up there
hoisted by that same wind
in the iciness in the grayness
encourages me or mocks me.

Between what's left of the ruins
and all this stuff to be built
in glass concrete steel
good place for gatherings and meetings.
And scowls and sarcasm from window to window
overlooking nothing
from facades in danger of collapse
from doors with nothing behind them
catapult me back
twenty years
onto a square in Venice
on the bouncing air of the Third Man –
as the television ghost for a brief moment
gambols backwards in replay...

                    here comes
the rain again
cold on the cold war, the face
loved for a few instants back then
soon cut off
behind a curtain of tears.

It Must Be the Boredom

of the long and scorching days
but little Laura
is really annoying today.
'Stop it,' I say, 'or else...'
twisting lightly her tiny arm
with repressed fierceness.

You don't hurt me you don't
hurt me, she dares me in a sing-song,
looking up at me,
petulant but already
on the verge of tears,
see I'm not even crying.

I see. But it's the dark
exterminating angel
that I see now
shining in his death
trappings
and turning to him in ecstasy
the Jewish child
invites him to the game
of massacre.

Sunday After the War

For two who meet again on a
Sunday after the war
can the desert of the sea
blossom anew?

'...love me,' he says, 'love me
back with all your strength with the strength
of vengeance for all these years...'
But

...in the early stages of the war
when Sundays were bland
desperation, deafening
of bells, residue
of smoke from the last
packet from Amsterdam
lingering off shore...

And they devour each other with their eyes,
they look for each other they hold hands
secretly on the damask linen of the table.

...sea solitary for years
of years computable in waves
arm of the sea stunned
by time frozen into space
by muteness...

Can the desert of the sea blossom anew?
But no, they sniff and study each other
gracious and tender almost
– he British she Flemish –
and then they hasten to work out the deal
not being even Sunday today.

Festival

In memory of L.S.

For how long have the times
been proving us wrong?
The hall gets more and more narrow
more packed with showcases with
vials patents orthopedic mannequins
adhesive labels
 – and within it the sprint
au ralenti where the born losers
vie for the jerseys
of those over the time limit
while those who had – or seemed to have –
dashed to the finish line
were pedaling backwards
along a wall of nausea.

Exterior Seen Again in a Dream

Never again – shreds of regiments –
would we be so much alike.

The clearing. This isn't peace.
Instead it would be
a carousel of winds a pasture of echoes
nothing but the hall of indifferent time
commonly called the end of youth.
And all around the oppressiveness of threadbare hills.

We walk along Algeria's wadis
gathering stones for dry walls
to shelter us from that autumn's rains.
Ranks abolished, uniforms tattered,
each returns with a stone in his hand.

Never again would we be so much alike.
– No peace without war – someone
leans out of the files coming and going.
There he goes again, the guy in charge of mortar fire
the biggest show-off the biggest braggart of all
as if he were
the head of the artilleries of all the Russias:
a certain Campana from Marradi,
expert in supplementary charges
poet in his spare time.

Peace was up there. On the hilltop.

A farmhouse
with its smoke lost between two clear patches
holds the promise of supper to a hunger of days.

Keep your chin up — winks that warlord —
you with your riflemen wouldn't you like
reinforcements of firepower?
We'll be sitting at the table before dark.

Drops of other rain pierced the sand
of the pre-desert shelf. *Night*
begins to fall on the two files
marching in opposite directions.
Up there
for a while longer
a last goodness illuminated things.

Giovanna and the Beatles

In the domestic muteness in the stillness
thinking she's alone and no one's listening
she breathes life into them again.
Along a streak of dust, leaving
behind them splinters of sound
in a sizzle
between astonished walls
go the well-loved Bugs.

Has *her* moment already passed with them?

Many times at the crossroads the switches of life
a subtle devil unexpectedly reappears
a shivery infiltrator
risen from nowhere under the guise of music
– a hill blazes with green again
a sea quickens –
unfailing seducer till
another music overcomes him, and us with him.

Every Time I Almost

slip through Luino again
on the square by the lake
bolting out of a store
a guy runs up to hug me
mumbling my mother's name.
Years ago, an older brother of his
used to do the same and now,
blossoming like then out of a clay wall
backwards along the train of the dead,
a hand suddenly wrenches us.

THREE

A Vacation Place

I

A many-leveled day, of high tide
– or in the lone sphere of blue.
A concave day which *is* before existing
on the reverse of summer the key of summer.
Of lone but triumphant summer spoils.
So day and key disappear
in the sulphur-like gush
of the thing that sinks into the sea.

White or not, the page is never really enticing in itself
less than ever here, between river and sea.
At the point, precisely, where a river runs into the sea.
Drafts on paper came from the other bank:
                        Sereni slender myth
thread of faithfulness not always youth is truth.

Tear up the white sheet you're holding in your hand.
There were no sheets or cards to play, it was true. Empty-handed,
without a message of reply, the ferryman returned from
            the other side.

A black man's river – a friend had promised –
one of America's fine black rivers.

This was the enticing fact. Opulent at the end of its run
pachydermic
            in certain hours of calm.
At first it was only dusty
reeds and, from the mouth, a coal-ship sea...
Who knows, peering from there name might be bound to
            thing
...(poetry on the vacation place).
Instead, after so many years that voice (it was a record)
from there, from the other bank, returns to tempt me.
In the evenings of dust and thirst
you could almost touch it, throat offered
to the wound of love upon the waters.
I will not write this story.

In the dark, amidst the leaves and canebrakes on the
            other bank,
they had discussions: on – it's just an example –
the retroactivity of error. But someone from the left
from the authentic left (I surprised myself wondering)
how does he get by, how does he live by the sea?
Although they were (not all) stronger rowers swimmers than I.
Year: 1951. Time of the world: Korea.
At times, I said hiding in the darkness, listening to you
            speak
awakens in me the black man I translated:
'You have sung, not spoken, nor searched the heart
of things: how can you know them?' the scribes
and orators say laughing when you...
But meanwhile the beautiful evening came undone upon
            the sea
and on the conversations the tables the reed enclosures

where they were dancing barefoot *el pueblo del alma mia*
the touch of the leaves appeared autumnal
turmoil and confusion on the left bank.

Up here there was the line, the Gothic's rightmost fringe,
you can still see – I still repeat it today
to the new arrivals with the monotony of a guide –
the positions of the Germans.
The Americans were shelling from the Fort
and in '51 the whining of a rare motorboat upriver
was still subtly alarming,
whatever went on the edge of the current
would be taken for the severed head of someone slain.
Still stunned by war, by that war,
only this united me to those speaking speaking
and still speaking on the wave of freedom...

II

Warm weather will be back.
The summer-colored bubble hits zero, it shrinks on the
                least
point of light where a couple slip away disappear in the
                evergreen
turning their back on my sickness
– and I on the sea – and a shot rings out
over the moment of blindness of silence.
Who fired who's firing in the clearing who
did that shoting in the thicket
between fields and wood along the rows?

From here I can' t see them,
only now I remember it's the first day of the hunting
    season.
I will not write this story, I repeat to myself,
if ever there was a story to tell.
                                    To hear
what the banks say about it,
(the parade of the banks
                        the banks
                            like brotherly propositions:
but they had foreseen me, they are silent, they invent
    nothing for me).
There doesn't seem to be anything else: my muteness is
    theirs.
But the dream of the reeds, the reeds in their dream
    determined
to make organ music with the river...
they are clues to other pulsations. I would like,
I alone the suspect,
I would like them to shine like proofs – I one among
    them.
One indeed lights up
at a late hour
                    the sneering of the moon still intact
inviolate
            on the black drift on the bustle of the waters.
On the undertow on the dark flowing
others light up on the opposite bank
– lamps or streetlights – even more unexpected,
human lights suddenly evoked – by what hands
on what terraces? – I take them to be signs agreed upon
I no longer know when or with whom

for new presences or returns.
'Let's say I had been waiting for you for years,'
my countersign comes from a lost code.
It will not cross the barrier of darkness and wind.
It will not cross the call already creased by winter
to an unfindable
                    ferryman.
So far away unmotivated motionless
beyond this acheron
those lights prove nothing, they call
neither me nor others.
Warm weather will be back.
Meanwhile a bevy of new girls in bloom darts by
leaving behind a tune:
mellow with a touch of bitterness
it returns between the sandy shores and the piers
like everything else here
it turns over, it curls. There, beyond the oleanders,
my shield from the sight of the sea,
there lies the provocation and the challenge –
a swimmer with his conjecturing
speech:
he confabulates behind a rock he ascends in circles he
            whirls away
mincing space in a deep-sea blueness
he has monologues dialogues far off making workshop
            noises –
a liquid workshop, an itinerant
swoon
of an August festival in a late-summer funeral –
                            and the glistening

wave, oceanic,
with flashes of cold on the oblique
breaker to glaze looks and voices in the Tyrrhenian
            summer...
here the poem breaks on the vacation place,
swept away by so much sea –
and having conquered the natural fear
here I am too on the side of the sea
becoming one with it
without ballast or fender of words,
cleaving the little gold left
on the small islands posthumous to daylight
amid the reefs already in shadows:
a while longer, and it's blackness once more.

III

'memory still full of desires'
you say you don't understand it – or, if you do, you do not love

Those two walking along the river, blue-and-white,
what are they ever saying to one another? Entwined or
            uncoupled
for years I have seen them pass
dancing in the reflection and the wind.
Standing on the dizzying heights, lingering ecstatic with
            her eyes
on the nearby hills and the more distant cliffs,
pointing against the light at cities
that maybe were and will never be –
'I'll give all this to you,' says the woman,
'if you'll adore me in submission.'
But the man, unequal to the dream and the oppression,

loses heart quickly, a music no longer lifts them.
                              And almost as if
none of these things had been, she goes back
to what she had been:
a shadow of the blood and of the mind,
and toward the shore
 in a short time they vanished.

It's the same old theater, it's the same old war.
Memory manufactures desires,
then it's left alone to bleed
on these multiple mirrors.
                              But look –
voices are returning from the river mouth – look how
         colors
change from hour to hour: from gray to green, from green
to the freshest blue. Love it then – from thing to thing
is the reply, from mirrored to mirroring –
love my remembering then
as it prances all around it sparkles it dissolves
it's all the possible, it's the sea.

                              IV

Never like this, said to himself the scribe,
hiding between the banks, never been
so tautological the work, but never
so trying either among so many wonders.
He watched the motorboat go off between two wings of
         coolness,
churn out up high, and it was already out of sight, in the
         deep blue,

rhapsodic dactylic daydreaming
perpetuating itself in the indistinctness of other summers.
He loved, should they ever serve the purpose,
those transients like living persons for a moment
and meanwhile the sea grew
upon the omission the gap the void
that settled between those two who had vanished
and the eyeing muttering animula there,
what had been a crystal just before
frosted over, it shattered,
and a glass speeding beyond the drift
beamed windward the last summer enigma.
The years, he kept on saying to himself, pass all at once,
and at a certain point they catch fire, I am
the guardian not of years but of moments
– and no one else who was supposed to come and was
expected no one else will come on the deserted waters.

(Could he have been anxious about fleeing Angelicas
or returning Helens? You might suppose so.
But don't believe – although this may seem like
a great love-sickness and feeds on it at times –
don't pay attention to the implorer on the banks,
he can be a good dissembler.
In fact, he was exhausting himself on a color
or rather on the name of the color to lay upon
the omission, the
gap, the void:
                amaranth,
light from spent stars that upon reaching us inflames us
or scatters upon breaking on a face
recognized at last, as the boat turns...)

Everything weighed anchor, everything
set sail under the glassy gaze
everything said farewell on the wave of the twentieth of
        August.
All that remained, caught in mid-air, was that Tyrrhenian
color, that name of bitter root,
the scribe's meager prey
dripping with more insomnia from the billows'
thousand suns of sparkling
insomnia.

V

Voices in the street are talking of the weather
that maybe is going to change, they are enraptured by the
        silver streaming
from crown to crown on the poplars combed backwards,
others arriving from the plain report
that summer is still ablaze with mirages,
neither a cicada nor a leaf has stopped.
The barrage of click-clacks goes off in several places and
        it spreads.

I thought, nothing worse than something
written which has the one who writes as hero, I mean
the one who writes as such, and his writer's doings and
        things as action.
There is no clearer indication of forthcoming shame:
someone observing himself as he writes himself
and then writing about this act of observing.
I have always said it and sometimes written:
Is it a sign, I wondered, that the reserves are dwindling,

that there remains, or there was, nothing else?
Was it perhaps, or is it, a necessary step? It would give
    me courage.
I watch the flotilla take refuge upriver driven by the storm.
The underbrush here used to be a retreat of painters,
gone today with part of the canebrakes: the times
have folded the easels thrown away the brushes torn the
    canvases to pieces.
Am I the surviving voyeur then, a stir
repressed between the banks, a fluvial metastasis?
one who dishes up copies of hours along the river,
of stasis and turbulence of the sea?
Someone comes, with the manners and accent of landing
    troops,
he stands before me wrapped in the unlikeliness of
    someone who,
having stayed at length in a place in a different time
and having repudiated it, shows up by chance again, for
    an hour.
'What are you doing still here in this tub?'
'Elio!' I blaze up again, 'Elio. But you loved
this place too if you used to say: a big kitchen,
or a big Brueghelian tailor-shop...' He thinks about it for
    a while:
'A kitchen?' I said. 'A kitchen.'
'With cooks and maids? Brueghelian?' 'Brueghelian.'
'Ah,' he says, 'and even a tailor shop? With people
    cutting and sewing?'
'With people cutting and sewing.' 'But,' he says. 'Where
    do you see them now?'
'Well,' I hedge, 'they still fish there, today, with casting nets.'
'But you,' he goes on, 'what are you doing in this tub?'

'I have an old score to settle,' I answer him.
'A score to settle? With words?' 'I hope not words alone.'
Oracular ironic polite, I sense he is about to disappear.
He jumps over ditches bores through hedges climbs over
       walls
and from the windy lookouts, already a long way off,
he doesn't spare me the derision
of places shouted as if in sleep, unreachable.

The hour of the time, the season no longer mild
resound with their deep echo, in the grayness.

VI

The shadow hovered just beneath the wave:
a skate, quite beautiful, violet in the turquoise
waving wing-like lobes.
Pierced, it gasped in pallor, it was lifeless,
marred by a small rose of blood
inside the basket, out of its element.
They explain to me that it's not always like this, not always
as I just saw it: that this and other deep-sea fish
mimic the sea-bed, the shoals, the currents,
their color darkening or paling as best suits them. I knew,
I know nothing of such things. Instinct would like to
       know them
merely by staying in their midst,
by living them, and not for amusement: only on this condition.
I would have liked to tell those experts about those other
       shadows and colors
of certain moments in us, how they cross us in our sleep
to sink in other timeless sleeps,

through what shoals and seabeds amid rekindlings and
        amnesias,
how many years are spent on them by the eye
intent upon the crossing and the sinking before they surface
frozen in the name which is not
the thing but only imitates it.
                            We wake up old
with that iridescent shadow in our head, sleepwalkers
among living beings descending
on a river of unperceived trifles that carry catastrophe in them
– and they don't see their loved ones grow and fade
        around them.
The interlocutor was right, the one
on the bank down there, who for a while has shown no
signs.
        But
'the sea turned hoary in an hour
in an hour finds its youth again,'
say the voices arriving in the storm's wake.

VII

Never so thick never
so thickly deliberating
barely out of the river mouth
in a circle the band of seagulls. One
breaks away in flight, it catches
something with a dive, it returns to the gathering.
You are already a winter sea:
estranged, as if withdrawn into itself.

To love not always is to know ('not always
youth is truth'), we see it late.

A stone, they explain to us,
is not so simple as it looks.
Even less so a flower.
One branches a cathedral within itself.
The other a paradise on earth.
Over both rises a Himalaya
of lives in motion.
                    Their profound design
was grasped
at the point where it becomes more manifest
– not a story belonging to me or others
not a love not even a poem
                    but a project
always in progress always
in fieri, to be a part of which
for once without humility or pride
knowing not to know.
On the reverse of summer.
In the sunny days of a December.

If it weren't so late.

But you, mirror now uniform and unremembering,
ready for new brushwood
smoke in the fields for new lights
at night from the plain for new
people pouring out of Carrara or Luni

really forget me now, don't flatter me any longer.

Niccolò

Fourth of September, someone
close to me has died today and with him kindness
once more and this time maybe for ever.

I was with others one last time on the sea
astonished that an immense, definitive
cloud did not settle on so many bright ghosts
in the fullness of the sky, but that only a vague mist
should descend between us, dust
left behind by summer
(it was there everywhere, we sensed it, on land and sea,
struggling to reach us, to break
the whitening diaphragm).
It will be no use looking for you on the furthest beaches
along the entire coastline as far as the one
they call the Coast of the Dead to know you won't come.

                              Now
that the world is being emptied of you and the truefalse
you of the poets becomes filled with you
now I know who was missing in the amaranth halo
what and who was deserting the waters
ten days ago
already showing hints of September. All inquiry suspended,
names retreat behind things
and the oleanders say no, they say no
stirred by the breeze.

And here we are again
with the sphere of blue, but isn't it
the usual hendyadis of sky and sea?
Stay with me then, you like it here,
and listen to me, as you know how.

1971

Fixity

From me to that shadow balanced between river and sea
only a streak of existence
from the river mouth against the light.
That man.
He mends nets, paints over a hull.
Things I can't do. Barely name them.
From me to him nothing else: a fixity.
Any redundancy gone elsewhere. Or spent.

FOUR

I Was Translating Char

I

In my own way, René Char,
with my usual means
on your material.

In the day that shines over the crumpled
evening his threshold of agony.
Or following with trepidation
the dusty strides
that raise a spring behind them.

A water ran, a hope
to drink all the green from it
under the dominion of spring.

II

Muezzin

From the highest tower
the chant of ill omen
wants us to repent.
For what wrongs yet, what sins?
It says that Allah is great
and at this time of night
in this dead hour
I believe it.

Luxor, 1973

III

A Lay Temple

From the clearing, the uneven ground
climbs solemnly
between steps and porticos
towards the gnats of death.

They become so streaked with gold
they will flash such empty eternity
from bank to bank
and for so long in the mind
absolute power
deposal and betrayal.

Valley of the Queens, 1973

IV

Vertical Village

Fresh with a recent passage
the vertical village replies
to the doubt of a misdirection:
with conversations of hedges
raving among bristles and velvets
creakings of doors
barely ajar rebounds
of echoes glimmerings cuckoos.

On the opposite ridge
a slash of light among the cliffs
turns a few stones into an acropolis.
The longed-for form
is a one-hour walk away
under the sun of the next province.

V

Hammered Slowness

When it's over it seems
as if you had known
the event beforehand
as if you had already lived through it
while it crashed on you
those thuds like a countdown
those clamors
bursting in the blood's caves.

To compensate for old damages years
of prostration the kiss
fell on the wound.

Soon it was clear even to me
that a judas was pressing against me
or rather a thais
disguised as a woodland rose.

VI

Nocturne

Down there, someone is talking about you:
the relentless full song
of the crickets and the starry
prairie of darkness.

It doesn't want you it banishes you
the majesty of night
gets rid of you
refuse of refuse.

VII

Madrigal to Nefertiti

Where can it be with whom the smile
that seems to know all about me
if it touches me
both past and future but not the present
if I try to say what waters
it becomes for me amidst palm-trees and dunes
and emerald shores
– and it tilts it on a yesterday
 of enchantments dross smoke
or defers it to a tomorrow
that won't belong to me
and if I speak to it it speaks of something else?

VIII

At the slightest chance
it would leap over a year
a resplendent coast
an airy valley
it comes to rest here
and it gets caught in the steps
in the lulls of the mind
the most resistant leaf – intermittent
longing: Vaucluse.

FIVE

Verano and Solstice

You who know everything of Rome, why
did you ever give that cemetery of yours
a Spanish name meaning summer?
(That's how, I didn't say it, spring carries its roots
into summer, in order to last,
and dies in it.)

The Roman summer lay before us
with its most vaporous
its most deadly calcination.

I'll make a note of it, he smiled, I'll tell you next time.

Tonight the invisible soloist cicada
of the last hour of light answers for him,
the inhabitant of the leaves that caught fire
in a day much too long:
this is el verano and the Verano,
it repeats with tireless fervor,
this is the summer of Rome of Spain of everywhere
this is the spring in summer,
the univocal the vermilion voice presses on, darkening
in all the returning Romes
of a few summers before.

Requiem

Irony withered courage faded
courage undone cheerfulness offended.
But so but then it's you
who's talking to me
from beneath the cascade of foliage and flowers,
really you answering?
                              Oh, the trappings
of beauty, the ornaments of death...
smiling or sneering
with what face under that mask?

First Fear

Every corner or alley every moment is right
for the killer who has been stalking me
night and day for years.
Shoot me shoot me, I tell him,
offering myself to his aim
front back sideways –
let's get it over with finish me off.
And in saying it I realize
I am speaking to myself alone.
                                   But
it's no use, it's no use. I haven't the strength
to be my own executioner.

Second Fear

There is nothing frightening
about the voice that calls
me really me
from the street below
during the night:
it's a brief reawakening of the wind,
a fleeting rain.
While it says my name it doesn't list
my faults, it doesn't reproach me for my past.
Softly (Vittorio,
Vittorio) it disarms me, against
myself it arms me.

Another Workplace

You're not going to tell me you
are you and I am I.
We have passed as years pass.
There is nothing of us here but the specimen
or rather the idly self-perpetuating
image –
and waters contemplate us and glass windows
they think of us in the future: headlong in the after,
ever fainter glosses,
multiple grains of us as we will have been.

Fall 1975

The Sickness of the Elm Tree

If it matters to you that it's still summer
there on the river bank the tree is scaling
the frailest leaves: rose-yellow
petals of unknown flowers
– and for future memory the motionless
evergreens.

But it matters more that people can walk in good cheer
that a city can run to the river that a seagull
venturing up here can unleaf
in a blaze of whiteness.

Guide me, variable star, for as long as you can...
– and the day dissolves the banks into honey and gold
it dissolves them again into an oily darkness
until the lights begin to teem.
                                    A droning
atom shoots out of that swarming,
with a dead aim
it hits me
where it stings and burns the most.

Come close to me, talk to me, tenderness,
I say turning to a
life so close to me till yesterday
today so far. Take out
this painful thorn,
memory:
its hunger is never appeased.

It's done, replies the murmuring
shadow in the last brightness,
now sleep, rest.
                    You have
taken out the prickle, but not
its fire, I sigh as I yield to it
already plunging into dream with it.

On the Climb

'In short, existence does not exist'
(the other one: 'read certain poets,
they will tell you
that it exists by not existing').
That odd dialogue climbed up and down
more than a by-road or two
on the way to the sea.
'Do the That-Is-to-Say boys
carry on like this
in the fierce scorching hour?'
I asked myself
trekking through that rocky ground.
It really makes no sense
except for certain bitter transients
when entire chunks of nature
become forever fixed in them,
frozen in their pupils.
                          But I
was the transient, it was me,
perplexed not really bitter.

The Knoll

What can be seen from here
– can you hear me? – from
the lookout of no return
– shadows of countrysides natural
stairs and what gurgling
of waters what flashes what blazing
colors what sumptuous tables –
is all that can be seen of you from here
and you don't know
the longer you stay.

Po Summer

Campitello Eremo Sustinente
places of discreet charms
multiplying the horizons of the suburbs
in walks outside the gate
of glances and whispers
among people bundled in the first
frost in the first fog
in a farewell step under a timid sun

today names of ghosts of the heat
through a dazzled and noiseless countryside
where a love sleeps
water dreaming water
for all that thirst.

In Parma with A.B.

I

Green mist tree
at the city's edge.
A misty green.
             What else?
I'd like to be something else.
I'd like to be you.
For so long so long ago
I would have liked to be like you
the poet of this city.
With fiery reasons at the time.
At the time unrequited.
Capable of saying nothing else today
that splash of green
becomes a steady pain.

II

If I say lighted window
if I say avenue soaked with rain
it's nothing, not even a song.
Had I been you, one of my evenings in Parma
would have had a voice even for me
and not
a tune smelling of dust and rain
crouching in the mind
between spring and summer.
And if it were a door facing other doors
as far as the one walled up at the end
which sooner or later will open?
More pain. In twinges.

III

Half-asleep beyond that door.
It happens. Sometimes.
That someone should speak of me
to me, very deep within me.
The old streetcar came down
from Marzolara to Parma
it whistled for a long time as it skirted the Baccanelli
greeting you absent
it spoke the certainty the horror of the end
it convinced of it that big summer sky.

To this shadow returns the horror of that void.

IV

Divine egoist, I know it's no use
asking you for help
I know you'd turn away.

Cherish, he says, this green
shadow and this hurt. Evasive,
moving aside, he covers it with one
of his acacia leaves –

                          invitation
to a feast being prepared for us
as vague as a cloud
straddling the Appennines.

The Cisa Highway

Ten years, not even time enough
for my father to die in me again
(he was lowered rudely
and a fogbank separated us forever).

Today, a kilometer away from the pass,
a long-haired dishevelled Erinys
waves a rag from the edge of a cliff,
extinguishes a day already extinct, and farewell.
You must know, someone said yesterday upon leaving me,
you must know it won't end here,
you must believe in that other life from moment to
        moment,
wait for it from coast to coast and it will come
as a summer returns from beyond the mountain pass.

So speaks the relapsing hope, it bites
in a watermelon the pulp of summer,
it sees each of those trees down there
perpetuate in itself its nymph,
and the tremor of a lake in the thirsty plain
behind the halo of echoes and mirages
turn Mantua into a Tenochtitlán.

From tunnel to tunnel, from dazzlement to blindness,
I hold out my hand. It returns empty.
I stretch out my arm. I clasp a shoulder of air.

You still don't know,
the sibyl hisses
in the din of the vaults,
she who longs to die more and more,
you still don't suspect
that of all the colors the strongest
the most indelible
is the color of the void?

Rimbaud

Let the pang of his name come for a moment
the drop that trickles from his name
inscribed in bright letters on that scorching wall.

Then he would hate me
the man with the soles of wind
for having believed it.

But the shadow, be it fox or mouse,
prowler of mastabas
darting away across our gaze
unrelated ignoring us in the waning light...

You thought it too.

He disappeared, he slipped away into his house
of stones and collapsing sand
and when the desert comes back to life
it hurls that name at us again in a long shiver.

Luxor, 1979

Luino-Luvino

As the wind swept
through deep or sunny valleys
I was just wondering if it was
silver of clouds or snow-clad sierra
things which still make winter gleam
when suddenly
the forelock fell over that face
it returned it to its phantom past
of wolfish epochs
and for a moment longer the eyes
showed through the thick hair
the teeth flashed
and soon took refuge in the pack
of lush places rocky names
hedging in all around
with their sound of harsh root
so soft at times
Valtravaglia Runo Dumenza Agra.

Progress

Those raven eyes, golden in the dying sunlight.
Beside her the city has suddenly
caught fire, it grows crimson,
it turns topaz and emerald.

From an old photo the dream
of the lamplighter aslant his bicycle
laughs at all this splendor,
if at his mere touch an entire city
should ever radiate simultaneously
to a century of lights
and all of us about to appear in it
– a fiery branch now
crumbling in its ashes.

Another Birthday

At July's end, when
from under the pergolas of a bar in San Siro
between railings and arches you catch a glimpse
of a few sectors of the sunlit stadium
when the huge empty bowl
is a bewildered mirror of squandered time
and it seems that a year is coming to die right there
and no one knows what else another year has in store
let's cross this threshold once again
as long as your heart can withstand those city billows
and a slate scatters the color of summer.

Notes

'Work in Progress I': *'e vuoti i letti etc.'* is the Italian adaptation of two lines from the poem 'These' by William Carlos William.

III: Ellis Island, entry station for immigrants, official and symbolic gate for millions of future American citizens from 1894 to 1954, the year in which the center was closed. The small island has since become a historical monument along with the nearby Statue of Liberty.

'In Venice with Biasion' had previously appeared in the non-commercial chapbook *In Venice with Biasion,* with six original etchings by Renzo Biasion.

'Revival': 'Opzione' (The Option) is the title of a sort of short story of mine written in the 1960s, published by Sheiwiller in 1964 and finally included in the first part of *Il sabato tedesco* (German Saturday) (Il Saggiatore, 1980). It is set in Frankfurt, as are the verses that allude to it.

'Sunday After the War': this is really the title of a book of short stories by Henry Miller, who is totally unrelated to the situation described here.

'A Vacation Place': it first appeared in Number 1, 1971, of *Almanacco dello specchio* (Ed. Mondadori), and it was later included in a small volume of *Pesce d'Oro* (Ed. Sheiwiller, 1973), accompanied by a long note of which I reproduce here only the explicatory part of some details:

I: 'the Negro I translated' is Jean-Joseph Rabèarivelo from Madagascar. The poem from which the words that follow are taken is entitled 'Your Work.'

III: the lines placed 'in limine' in this section are mine and belong to a poem which remained unfinished several years ago. The latter in turn referred to another old poem of mine

'Gli squali' ('The Sharks') in *Gli strumenti umani*.

'All this... you'll adore me' is a not entirely unjustified feminine appropriation of the words with which, according to Matthew, the devil had tempted Jesus.

'And almost as if... they vanished': this time the appropriation is the author's, from the tale of Nastagio degli Onesti in the *Decameron*.

V: Elio, there is almost no need to say it, is Elio Vittorini, who reappears in the place we once frequented together.

'I Was Translating Char' are moments of life, or rather the recovery (not exercises, not 'studies') of a time when I was doing this type of work.

'Verano and Solstice': the association of Verano, Rome's cemetery, with *el verano*, meaning summer in Spanish, is totally arbitrary; somewhat less so is finding the Latin term for spring (*ver*) in the root of the Spanish name for summer.

'Cisa Highway': the section mentioned is the La Spezia-Parma, in the direction of the Po valley.

'Tenochtitlán,' today Mexico City. Once enlivened by a lake, it was the capital of the Aztec kingdom before the Spanish conquest: a city happy in memory, as always after the catastrophe.

'Rimbaud': anyone who has visited the Luxor temple might have noticed that writing. As far as I know, there are no proofs or documents relative to the passage in that place of '*l'homme aux semelles de vent,*' at any rate improbable author of the writing. Mastaba is the modern name of ancient Egyptian tombs in the form of a truncated pyramid.

'Luino-Luvino': in the last century Luvino was the name of Luino, my birthplace.

Afterword

Enticing and dissuading nature. Omnipresent and unreachable beauty. The world of man that asks for and avoids judgment, and never receives a final sentence. Fluctuating and changeable life.

Montaigne

Born in Luino, on the shores of Lago Maggiore, on July 27, 1913, from a Lombard mother and a father, a customs officer, who had come from the South, Vittorio Sereni graduated from the State University of Milan with a thesis on the poetry of Guido Gozzano. Initially, he devoted himself to a teaching career, but was soon drawn to the ideological and literary currents of contemporary Milan. He contributed in fact to reviews such as *Corrente, Campo di Marte* and *Letteratura*. In 1937 he published his first two poems in the Florentine review Frontespizio.

Sereni took part in War World II fighting as an infantry officer in Greece and Sicily: it was indeed at the Trapani front that he was taken prisoner by the Allies. After the war he returned to Milan, where he briefly took up teaching again, only to leave it in 1952 to work as chief of Pirelli's press office and finally as the literary director for Mondadori Publishing. The latter position, which he himself defined as 'editorial-literary,' allowed him to pursue his own artistic interests and to establish important contacts with famous figures in the world of culture. Sereni was also editor of *La Rassegna d'Italia*, and from 1950 to 1951 wrote literary criticism for *Milano-Sera*.

The writer received many literary awards for his work, among which the Free Press Award in 1956, the Montefeltro Award in 1965, the Bagutta Award in 1981, and finally, in 1981, *Variable Star* won the Viareggio Award for poetry. Having retired several years earlier from active employment at Mondadori, Sereni continued to work tirelessly till the end in various sectors of Italian culture. He died of cardiac arrest on February 10, 1983.

Sereni's political experience emerges in the 1930s at the height of Hermeticism. While he himself recognized his initial 'dependence' on the school, he was soon to abandon its solipsistic tendencies in favor of a more realistic and personal kind of poetry. Drawing inspiration from Montale's lesson of a type of 'poetry yielding to objects' and following the directives of the 'Lombard line' – the geographical-literary demarcation suggested by Carlo Bo – Sereni found himself in favor of a poetry *in re*, as Luciano Anceschi defines it, that is, a kind of poetry 'that becomes flesh, that can be touched.' He rejected therefore the metaphysical refinements and aristocratic extremism of the Florentine Hermetics who, in their commitment to the absolute search for the essential word, denied any contact with reality.

Sereni's poetic *iter* is outlined in the four collections of poems: *Frontiera* (Frontier, 1941), *Diario d'Algeria* (Algerian Diary, 1947), *Gli strumenti umani* (Human Instruments, 1965), *Stella variabile* (Variable Star, 1981). The poems of *Frontiera*, having as backdrop the idyllic landscape of the Lombard lakes, give voice to youthful doubts and desires. The term 'frontier' underlines the poet's aspiration toward a more authentic world, free from fear and desperation.

In *Diario d'Algeria* the writer comes to terms with the reality of war and defeat. One of the most significant themes in this collection is represented by the dialectics of alienation and commitment: the events of War World II have kept the poet in a state of forced 'absence' – as a prisoner of war – but in almost every poem of the *Diario* one can perceive a deep and impassioned sense of commitment and participation in the common drama of suffering. *Gli strumenti umani* deal with the difficult period of the aftermath of the war, from 1945 to 1965, with its state of anxiety, on a 'generational' level, of existential and civil crisis and of confusion in the face of a constantly changing social reality.

Variable Star

Variable Star, Vittorio Sereni's last book of verse and the one perhaps containing, as the author himself underlined, his best poetry, was published by Garzanti in December 1981. In the text, the poet's discourse centers on 'variations' of a few fundamental themes, among which predominates, from the very first composition, the theme of death: 'Those thoughts of yours of calamity / and catastrophe / in the house where you have / come to stay, already / inhabited by the idea / of your having come here / to die...' ('Those Thoughts of Yours of Calamity'). In these lines we find the frequent use of words like 'emptiness,' 'shadow,' 'night,' 'sleep,' 'silence,' that reiterate the idea of this daily meditation on death: 'new shadows that I glimpse at without seeing / now disquiet me' ('Work in Progress'), or 'It must be that there are lives like dead leaves' ('Work in Progress'), or further on: 'The silence / fermented in the darkness of the room' ('Women'). The constant thoughts of death are accompanied, more generally, by troubled visions of an increasingly threatened reality: hence the ambiguous signs in New York 'small swastikas' or 'old Indian motifs' ('Work in Progress'); the 'waters perpetually troubled,' the 'distancing black waters' of Venice ('In Venice with Biasion'); the extended hand that 'From tunnel to tunnel, from dazzlement to blindness / ...returns empty' ('Cisa Highway').

But these signs of disorientation and premonition, these thoughts and meditations on death are counterbalanced, in an almost oscillatory movement of lights and shadows, by inventive – I would say solar – outbursts, attesting on the one hand a vitalistic energy very much present in the poet, and on the other the great transfiguring power of this poetry: '...What came / to life – I suddenly able to see in the air's slow brightening – / was a throng of daisies and buttercups out there' ('In an Empty

House'); and again: '...The spike / of his solar bread soars / over shapeless outlines / over setting domes and peaks' ('In Venice with Biasion'); we then have the transfiguring image of stones and flowers that carry in them 'a project' of life ('A Vacation Place'), the dazzling vision of that 'seagull...' that 'can unleaf in a blaze of whiteness' ('The Sickness of the Elm Tree') or of the city that lighting up 'grows crimson / it turns topaz, it turns emerald' ('Progress').

As was previously mentioned, this poetry tends to resolve itself into an oscillatory movement of lights and shadows, a movement which on the one hand reflects the changeability of reality – it is not by chance that Sereni inserts on the inside cover, in an almost programmatic way, this line from Montaigne: 'Fluctuating and changeable life' – and on the other, the contrasts and changes in the poet's spirit. The inspiration of this poetry is thus rooted in an existential dialectics centered on an oxymoronic metaphor, made of opposites: it is a solarity, an enlightening and enlightened view of life that, through a myriad intermediate stages, borders on its opposite, namely on shadow, non-existence, death.

Of the five sections into which Variable Star is divided, the third, containing only three poems – 'A Vacation Place,' 'Niccolò,' and 'Fixity' – is perhaps, as also noted by Lento Gioffi, the most 'compact' and uniform, and acquires a key position in the economy of the book, not so much for the setting – the Tyrrhenian coast, specifically Bocca di Magra – or for the season – a summer waning into Autumn (in other words, a 'reverse' of summer), but because we find in it some of the fundamental themes of Sereni's poetry.

Above all, we find the theme of friendship, associated with that of the conversation with the dead; with Elio Vittorini: 'Someone comes, with the manners and accent of landing troops' ('A Vacation Place'); and with Niccolò Gallo: 'Fourth of September, someone / close to me has died today and with him kindness / once more' ('Niccolò'); we also find the memory of war: 'Up here there was the line, the outermost right fringe of the Gothic, / you can still see... / the positions of the Germans' ('A Vacation Place').

Then there is the discourse on poetry, begun in *Gli immediati dintorni* (The Immediate Surroundings) and taken up again in *Gli strumenti umani* (Human Instruments): the critical and self-critical sense of the function of poetry, the constant and perplexed self-questioning over the value of poetry, over the plausibility of a story to write or not to write. It is the poet's task to ensure that the '...name be bound to thing' (poetry on the vacation place)' ('A Vacation Place'). It is not an easy task: there is, first of all, the constant self-questioning before the 'white page' that rarely is 'enticing'; in addition, there is the realization on the part of the author, in his reluctant and humble perplexity, of a lack of knowledge: 'I knew, I know / nothing of such things' ('A Vacation Place').

But despite all this, 'the scribe' will not abandon his 'meager prey' and will continue to pursue with great effort that reality from which he has always drawn the vital lymph for his poetry. Despite its changeability, despite its 'amaranth' color - or rather the color to 'lay / upon the omission, the / failing, / the void,' in it he glimpses : 'A stone... / a flower. / One branches a cathedral within itself. / The other a paradise on earth,' or rather 'projects ...always in progress / always in fieri, to be a part of which / for once without humility or pride / knowing not to know' ('A Vacation Place').

Answering a question on the meaning of the title 'Variable Star,' the poet observed: 'It has an allusive value,... but it is better for each individual to look for a meaning,' thus confirming the conviction that poetry, like a shining star, even if variable, can still guide man in a personal search for truth.

Laura Baffoni Licata

Québec, Canada
1999